# Sorting through Spring

written by

Lizann Flatt

illustrated by

Ashley Barron

Owl
kids

Do you think that math matters to the animals and plants?

What if nature knew numbers like you?

Let's look at the spring.

Imagine what patterns and sorting could do!

What if raindrops weren't random
dropping down from the sky?
What if rain had a rhythm,
or a beat to repeat?

*Plop drop plop-plop. Plop drop plop-plop.*
Could that steady wet sound
awaken worms underground?

**Can you make up a
clapping rhythm for rain?**

As more raindrops flop to the *plop drop plop-plop*,
they gather in muddled wet, rhythmic rain huddles
while worms wiggle around on the ground.

**Do you see a pattern to the worms on the ground?**

Would prairie chickens practice their moves so they match?

*Woo-woo flap, stampity stomp-stamp.*

**Can you perform this pattern?**

stampity

stomp – stamp

Would birds arrange eggs
so the tree branches balanced?

If 8 hummingbird eggs equal
4 robin eggs, which two ratios
are correct: 3 to 1, 8 to 4,
5 to 1, 2 to 1?

Would the smelt in their schools
learn about pattern rules?

Can you see two
pattern rules here?

Would milk snakes like these,
when they need to feed,
find food that fits with their patterns?

**Which egg shows the shape
that comes first in each
milk snake's pattern?**

Could flowers only grow
in set patterns, row by row?

**Which rows make an
ABA, ABA pattern?
What other patterns
do you see?**

When their antlers fall off,
would the caribou take care
to place them in proper piles?

Into which colored pile would you sort the antlers below? How else could you sort them?

Could cottontails claim that they're cramped in their nests?

Might some feel more comfortable than the rest?

**Which nests hold a number of babies that is greater than 5? Less than 5? Equal to 5?**

If the peepers took a poll on who sings the best,
would the winner sing solo? Would he silence the rest?

**Which of the three spring peepers has
the most votes? Match fingers to find out.
Can you create a chart to show your findings?**

Could the fox family figure
what Father's bringing home for dinner?

Is their dinner impossibly,
unlikely, likely, or certainly a vole?
A gray squirrel? A rabbit? A cat?

What if mosquitoes were mistaken
and ignored the data taken?

According to the graph, where should
the mosquitoes lay their eggs?

Morning comes before noon, and noon comes before night.

If the pattern was changed, wouldn't that be a sight?

Maybe noon, morning, night?

That wouldn't be right!

The sun sets a pattern of light we all like:

morning, noon, night ... morning, noon, night.

**How can you tell it's morning?**

How can you tell it's afternoon?

So ... does nature know numbers?
No way! That's not true.
The only creature to need numbers?
Actually, just you!

How can you tell it's night?

# Nature Notes

After lying dormant through the winter, worms begin to eat and move around again when the ground thaws in the spring. They come up to the surface when it rains so that they can move over the ground to new areas without drying out.

Every spring in breeding grounds called leks, prairie chicken males perform a dance to attract females. Males use their orange neck sacs to make a "woo-woo" sound that acts as their mating call. They also stamp their feet, strut, and fly at one another!

Robins lay blue eggs. There are usually four eggs to a nest. Ruby-throated hummingbirds usually lay two pea-sized white eggs in a nest. One robin egg is about the same size as two hummingbird eggs.

In early spring, when the lake ice is breaking up, schools of smelt swim at night from shallow ocean coasts or big lakes up into small creeks and rivers to lay their eggs. A female smelt can lay as many as 93,000 eggs!

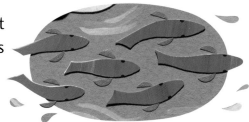

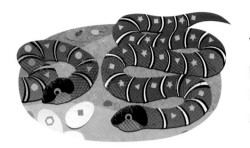

The milk snake's colorful skin pattern makes it look like some types of poisonous snakes. This fools predators into not eating it. Milk snakes eat rodents, birds, other snakes, and the eggs from birds and snakes. In the spring, they come out of their winter dens after hibernating in groups.

Spring rain soaks into the ground and makes flowers grow. Bulbs, a type of plant stem that stores food and water, bloom into flowers. Seeds swell up and sprout. Trees and shrubs also absorb water, and their leaves bud and their flowers bloom.

Female caribou grow antlers just like male caribou do. Most males lose their antlers by November, but mother caribou don't lose theirs until the spring, after their babies are born. Every year, caribou grow a new set of antlers.

Cottontail rabbits have babies in nests on the ground. The babies are born helpless, but they can look after themselves after four or five weeks. When being hunted, cottontail rabbits hop away in a zigzag pattern to confuse their enemies.

**Spring peepers** are tiny frogs that live in moist wooded areas. The males call or sing a peeping noise to attract mates. Thousands of peepers singing together can make a deafening noise on spring nights! They lay eggs in temporary spring woodland ponds, puddles, and marshes. They can climb plants and trees easily with their sticky toe pads.

**Red foxes** use their senses of sight, hearing, and smell to hunt. When a mother fox has babies in the spring, the father fox hunts for the family. When the babies are a bit older, the parents take turns hunting for themselves, and both bring back prey for the babies.

**Mosquitoes** lay their eggs in water or moist places. When the eggs hatch, the larvae grow in the water. When fully grown, the mosquitoes can fly, live on land, and eat plant nectar. Female mosquitoes need blood to develop their eggs. They get this blood by biting animals and people.

As the Earth moves around the **Sun**, the amount of sunlight we can see changes, giving us morning, noon, and night. But some places on Earth, such as the Arctic, have long periods of darkness or long periods of light.

*The author wishes to acknowledge the support of the Ontario Arts Council through the Writers' Reserve program.*

Owlkids Books Inc.
10 Lower Spadina Avenue, Suite 400, Toronto, Ontario M5V 2Z2
www.owlkidsbooks.com

Distributed in Canada by University of Toronto Press
5201 Dufferin Street, Toronto, Ontario M3H 5T8

Distributed in the United States by Publishers Group West
1700 Fourth Street, Berkeley, California 94710

Library and Archives Canada Cataloguing in Publication

　　Sorting through spring / written by Lizann Flatt ; illustrated by Ashley Barron.

(Math in nature ; 2)
Issued also in electronic format.
ISBN 978-1-926973-59-3

　　1. Mathematics--Juvenile literature.  2. Nature--Juvenile literature.
3. Spring--Juvenile literature.  I. Barron, Ashley  II. Title.
III. Series: Flatt, Lizann.  Math in nature ; 2.

QA40.5.F53 2012　　　　　j510　　　　　C2012-904858-5

Library of Congress Control Number: 2012945652

Design: Claudia Dávila

Canadian Heritage　Patrimoine canadien

Canada

Ontario
Ontario Media Development Corporation
Société de développement de l'industrie des médias de l'Ontario

Canada Council for the Arts　Conseil des Arts du Canada

ONTARIO ARTS COUNCIL
CONSEIL DES ARTS DE L'ONTARIO

We acknowledge the financial support of the Canada Council for the Arts, the Ontario Arts Council, the Government of Canada through the Canada Book Fund (CBF) and the Government of Ontario through the Ontario Media Development Corporation's Book Initiative for our publishing activities.

Manufactured by C&C Joint Printing Co., (Guangdong) Ltd.
Manufactured in Shenzhen, China, in September 2012
Job #HM5050

A　　B　　C　　D　　E　　F

OWL kids　Publisher of Chirp, chickaDEE and OWL
　　　　　www.owlkidsbooks.com

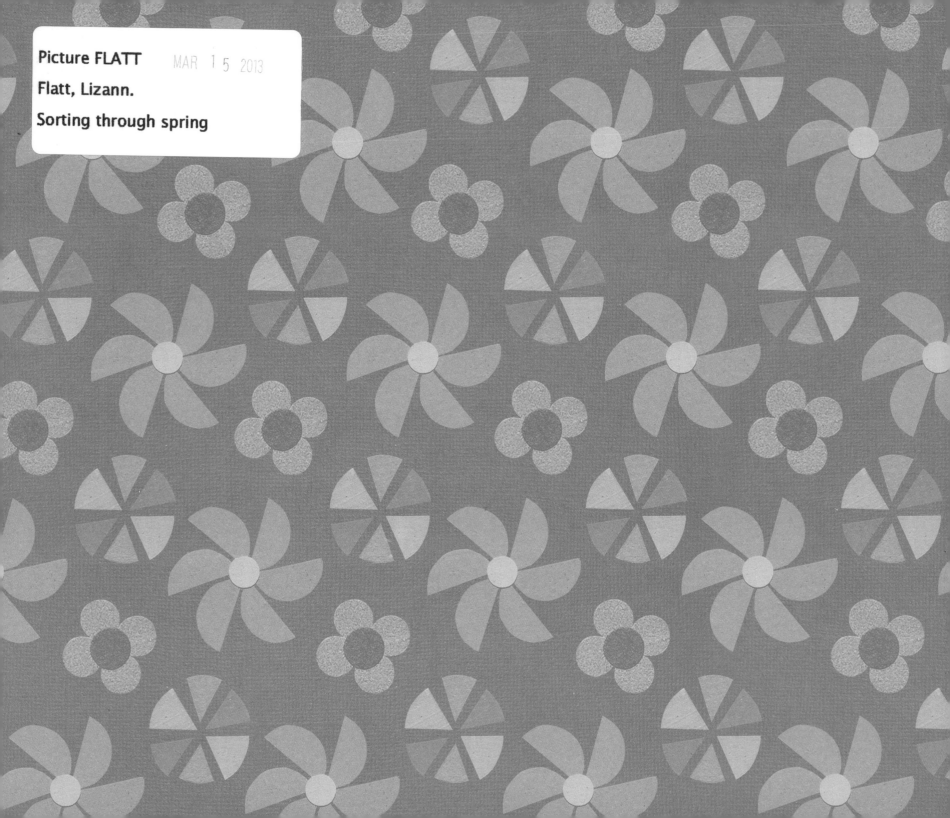